Books by TRUMAN CAPOTE

ONE CHRISTMAS

ONE

CHRISTMAS

Truman Capote

RANDOM HOUSE

NEW YORK

Portions of this work were previously published in the Ladies' Home Journal.
This work was originally published in 1983 by Random House, Inc.

Library of Congress Cataloging in Publication Data
Capote, Truman, 1924–
One Christmas.
1. Christmas stories.   I. Title.
PS3505.A5905   1983   813'.54   83-3177
ISBN 0-679-44346-0

Typography adapted from a design by George Salter
Manufactured in the United States of America
9 8 7 6 5 4 3 2
RANDOM HOUSE 1994 EDITION

for Gloria Dumphy

ONE CHRISTMAS

First, a brief autobiographical pro-logue. My mother, who was exceptionally intelligent, was the most beautiful girl in Alabama. Everyone said so, and it was true; and when she was sixteen she mar-ried a twenty-eight-year-old businessman who came from a good New Orleans family. The marriage lasted a year. My mother was too young to be a mother or a wife; she was also too ambitious—she wanted to go to college and to have a career. So she left her husband; and as for what to do with me, she deposited me in the care of her large Alabama family.

Over the years, I seldom saw either of my parents. My father was occupied in New Orleans, and my mother, after graduating from college, was making a success for herself in New York. So far as I was concerned, this was not an unpleasant situation. I was happy where I was. I had many kindly relatives, aunts and uncles and cousins, particularly *one* cousin, an elderly, white-haired, slightly crippled woman named Sook. Miss Sook Faulk. I had other friends, but she was by far my best friend.

It was Sook who told me about Santa Claus, his

flowing beard, his red suit, his jangling present-filled sled, and I believed her, just as I believed that everything was God's will, or the Lord's, as Sook always called Him. If I stubbed my toe, or fell off a horse, or caught a good-sized fish at the creek—well, good or bad, it was all the Lord's will. And that was what Sook said when she received the frightening news from New Orleans: My father wanted me to travel there to spend Christmas with him.

I cried. I didn't want to go. I'd never left this small, isolated Alabama town surrounded by forests and farms and rivers. I'd never gone to sleep without Sook combing her fingers through my hair and kissing me good-night. Then, too, I was afraid of strangers, and my father was a stranger. I had seen him several times, but the memory was a haze; I had no idea what he was like. But, as Sook said: "It's the Lord's will. And who knows, Buddy, maybe you'll see snow."

Snow! Until I could read myself, Sook read me many stories, and it seemed a lot of snow was in almost all of them. Drifting, dazzling fairytale flakes. It was something I dreamed about; something magical and mysterious that I wanted to see and feel and touch. Of course I never had, and neither had Sook; how could we, living in a hot place like Alabama? I don't know why she thought I would see snow in New Orleans, for New Orleans is even hotter. Never mind.

She was just trying to give me courage to make the trip.

I had a new suit. It had a card pinned to the lapel with my name and address. That was in case I got lost. You see, I had to make the trip alone. By bus. Well, everybody thought I'd be safe with my tag. Everybody but me. I was scared to death; and angry. Furious at my father, this stranger, who was forcing me to leave home and be away from Sook at Christmastime.

It was a four-hundred-mile trip, something like that. My first stop was in Mobile. I changed buses there, and rode along forever and forever through swampy lands and along seacoasts until we arrived in a loud city tinkling with trolley cars and packed with dangerous foreign-looking people.

That was New Orleans.

And suddenly, as I stepped off the bus, a man swept me in his arms, squeezed the breath out of me; he was laughing, he was crying—a tall, good-looking man, laughing and crying. He said: "Don't you know me? Don't you know your daddy?"

I was speechless. I didn't say a word until at last, while we were riding along in a taxi, I asked: "Where is it?"

"Our house? It's not far—"

"Not the house. The snow."

"What snow?"

"I thought there would be a lot of snow."

He looked at me strangely, but laughed. "There never has been any snow in New Orleans. Not that I heard of. But listen. Hear that thunder? It's sure going to rain!"

I don't know what scared me most, the thunder, the sizzling zigzags of lightning that followed it—or my father. That night, when I went to bed, it was still raining. I said my prayers and prayed that I would soon be home with Sook. I didn't know how I could ever go to sleep without Sook to kiss me good-night. The fact was, I couldn't go to sleep, so I began to wonder what Santa Claus would bring me. I wanted a pearl-handled knife. And a big set of jigsaw puzzles. A cowboy hat

17

with matching lasso. And a B.B. rifle to shoot spar-
rows. (Years later, when I did have a B.B. gun, I shot
a mockingbird and a bobwhite, and I can never forget
the regret I felt, the grief; I never killed another thing,
and every fish I caught I threw back into the water.)
And I wanted a box of crayons. And, most of all, a ra-
dio but I knew that was impossible : I didn't know ten
people who had radios. Remember, this was the De-
pression, and in the Deep South houses furnished with
radios or refrigerators were rare.

My father had both. He seemed to have everything
—a car with a rumble seat, not to mention an old, pink
pretty little house in the French Quarter with iron-lace
balconies and a secret patio garden colored with flow-

18

ers and cooled by a fountain shaped like a mermaid. He also had a half-dozen, I'd say full-dozen, lady friends. Like my mother, my father had not remarried; but they both had determined admirers and, willingly or not, eventually walked the path to the altar—in fact, my father walked it six times.

So you can see he must have had charm; and, indeed, he seemed to charm most people—everybody except me. That was because he embarrassed me so, always hauling me around to meet his friends, everybody from his banker to the barber who shaved him every day. And, of course, all his lady friends. And the worst part: All the time he was hugging and kissing me and bragging about me. I felt so ashamed. First of all, there was nothing to brag about. I was a real country boy. I believed in Jesus, and faithfully said my prayers. I knew Santa Claus existed. And at home in Alabama, except to go to church, I never wore shoes; winter or summer.

It was pure torture, being pulled along the streets of New Orleans in those tightly laced, hot as hell, heavy as lead shoes. I don't know what was worse—the shoes or the food. Back home I was used to fried chicken and collard greens and butter beans and corn bread and other comforting things. But these New Orleans restaurants! I will never forget my first oyster, it was like a bad dream sliding down my throat; decades passed before I swallowed another. As for all that spicy Creole cookery—just to think of it gave me heartburn. No sir, I hankered after biscuits right from the stove and milk fresh from the cows and homemade molasses straight from the bucket.

My poor father had no idea how miserable I was, partly because I never let him see it, certainly never told him; and partly because, despite my mother's protest, he had managed to get legal custody of me for this Christmas holiday.

He would say: "Tell the truth. Don't you want to come and live here with me in New Orleans?"

"I can't."

"What do you mean you can't?"

"I miss Sook. I miss Queenie; we have a little rat terrier, a funny little thing. But we both love her."

He said: "Don't you love me?"

I said: "Yes." But the truth was, except for Sook and Queenie and a few cousins and a picture of my beautiful mother beside my bed, I had no real idea of what love meant.

I soon found out. The day before Christmas, as we were walking along Canal Street, I stopped dead still, mesmerized by a magical object that I saw in the window of a big toy store. It was a model airplane large enough to sit in and pedal like a bicycle. It was green and had a red propeller. I was convinced that if you pedaled fast enough it would take off and fly! Now wouldn't that be something! I could just see my cousins standing on the ground while I flew about among the clouds. Talk about green! I laughed; and laughed and laughed. It was the first thing I'd done that made my father look confident, even though he didn't know what I thought was so funny.

That night I prayed that Santa Claus would bring me the airplane.

My father had already bought a Christmas tree, and we spent a great deal of time at the five 'n' dime picking out things to decorate it with. Then I made a mistake. I put a picture of my mother under the tree. The moment my father saw it he turned white and began to tremble. I didn't know what to do. But he did. He went to a cabinet and took out a tall glass and a bottle. I recognized the bottle because all my Alabama uncles had plenty just like it. Prohibition moonshine. He filled the tall glass and drank it with hardly a pause. After that, it was as though the picture had vanished.

And so I awaited Christmas Eve, and the always exciting advent of fat Santa. Of course, I had never seen a weighted, jangling, belly-swollen giant flop down a chimney and gaily dispense his largesse under a Christmas tree. My cousin Billy Bob, who was a mean little runt but had a brain like a fist made of iron, said it was a lot of hooey, there was no such creature.

"My foot!" he said. "Anybody would believe there was any Santa Claus would believe a mule was a horse." This quarrel took place in the tiny courthouse square. I said: *"There is a Santa Claus because what he*

24

does is the Lord's will and whatever is the Lord's will is the truth." And Billy Bob, spitting on the ground, walked away: "Well, looks like we've got another preacher on our hands."

I always swore I'd never go to sleep on Christmas Eve, I wanted to hear the prancing dance of reindeer on the roof, and to be right there at the foot of the chimney to shake hands with Santa Claus. And on this particular Christmas Eve, nothing, it seemed to me, could be easier than staying awake.

My father's house had three floors and seven rooms, several of them huge, especially the three leading to the patio garden: a parlor, a dining room and a "musical" room for those who liked to dance and play and deal cards. The two floors above were trimmed with lacy balconies whose dark green iron intricacies were delicately entwined with bougainvillea and rippling vines of scarlet spider orchids—a plant that resembles lizards flicking their red tongues. It was the kind of house best displayed by lacquered floors and some wicker here, some velvet there. It could have been mistaken for the house of a rich man; rather, it was the place of a man with an appetite for elegance. To a poor (but happy) barefoot boy from Alabama it was a mystery how he managed to satisfy that desire.

But it was no mystery to my mother, who, having graduated from college, was putting her magnolia delights to full use while struggling to find in New York a truly suitable fiancé who could afford Sutton Place apartments and sable coats. No, my father's resources were familiar to her, though she never mentioned the matter until many years later, long after she had acquired ropes of pearls to glisten around her sable-wrapped throat.

She had come to visit me in a snobbish New England boarding school (where my tuition was paid by her rich and generous husband), when something I said tossed her into a rage; she shouted: "So you don't know how he lives so well? Charters yachts and cruises the Greek Islands? His *wives*! Think of the whole long string of them. All widows. All rich. *Very* rich. And all much older than he. Too old for any sane young man to marry. That's why you are his only child. And that's why I'll never have another child—I was too young to have any babies, but he was a beast, he wrecked me, he ruined me—"

Just a gigolo, everywhere I go, people stop and stare . . . Moon, moon over Miami . . . This is my first affair, so please be kind . . . Hey, mister, can you spare a dime? . . . Just a gigolo, everywhere I go, people stop and stare . . .

All the while she talked (and I tried not to listen, because by telling me my birth had destroyed her, *she* was destroying me), these tunes ran through my head, or tunes like them. They helped me not to hear her, and they reminded me of the strange haunting party my father had given in New Orleans that Christmas Eve.

The patio was filled with candles, and so were the three rooms leading off it. Most of the guests were gathered in the parlor, where a subdued fire in the fireplace made the Christmas tree glitter; but many others were dancing in the music room and the patio to music from a wind-up Victrola. After I had been introduced to the guests, and been made much of, I had been sent upstairs; but from the terrace outside my French-shuttered bedroom door, I could watch all the party, see all the couples dancing. I watched my father waltz a graceful lady around the pool that surrounded the mermaid fountain. She *was* graceful, and dressed in a wispy silver dress that shimmered in the candlelight; but she was old—at least ten years older than my father, who was then thirty-five.

I suddenly realized my father was by far the youngest person at his party. None of the ladies, charming as they were, were any younger than the willowy waltzer in the floating silver dress. It was the same with the men, so many of whom were smoking sweet-smelling Havana cigars; more than half of them were old enough to be my father's father.

Then I saw something that made me blink. My father and his agile partner had danced themselves into a niche shadowed by scarlet spider orchids; and they were embracing, kissing. I was so startled, I was so *irate*, I ran into my bedroom, jumped into bed and pulled the covers over my head. What would my nice-looking young father want with an old woman like that! And why didn't all those people downstairs go home so Santa Claus could come? I lay awake for hours listening to them leave, and when my father said good-bye for the last time, I heard him climb the stairs and open my door to peek at me; but I pretended to be asleep.

Several things occurred that kept me awake the whole night. First, the footfalls, the noise of my father running up and down the stairs, breathing heavily. I had to see what he was up to. So I hid on the balcony among the bougainvillea. From there, I had a complete view of the parlor and the Christmas tree and the fireplace where a fire still palely burned. Moreover, I could see my father. He was crawling around under the tree arranging a pyramid of packages. Wrapped in purple paper, and red and gold and white and blue, they rustled as he moved them about. I felt dizzy, for what I saw forced me to reconsider everything. If these were presents intended for me, then obviously they had not been ordered by the Lord and delivered by Santa Claus; no, they were gifts bought and wrapped by my father. Which meant that my rotten little cousin Billy Bob and other rotten kids like him weren't lying when they taunted me and told me there was no Santa

32

Claus. The worst thought was: Had Sook known the truth, and lied to me? No, Sook would never lie to me. She *believed*. It was just that—well, though she was sixty-something, in some ways she was at least as much of a child as I was.

I watched until my father had finished his chores and blown out the few candles that still burned. I waited until I was sure he was in bed and sound asleep. Then I crept downstairs to the parlor, which still reeked of gardenias and Havana cigars.

I sat there, thinking: Now I will have to be the one to tell Sook the truth. An anger, a weird malice was spiraling inside me: It was not directed towards my father, though he turned out to be its victim.

When the dawn came, I examined the tags attached to each of the packages. They all said: "For Buddy." All but one, which said: "For Evangeline." Evangeline was an elderly colored woman who drank Coca-Cola all day long and weighed three hundred pounds; she was my father's housekeeper—she also mothered him. I decided to open the packages: It was Christmas morning, I was awake, so why not? I won't bother to describe what was inside them: just shirts and sweaters and dull stuff like that. The only thing I appreciated was a quite snazzy cap-pistol. Somehow I got the idea it would be fun to waken my father by firing it. So I did. *Bang. Bang. Bang.*

He raced out of his room, wild-eyed.

34

Bang. Bang. Bang.

"Buddy—what the hell do you think you're doing?"

Bang. Bang. Bang.

"Stop that!"

I laughed. "Look, Daddy. Look at all the wonderful things Santa Claus brought me."

Calm now, he walked into the parlor and hugged me. "You like what Santa Claus brought you?"

I smiled at him. He smiled at me. There was a tender lingering moment, shattered when I said: "Yes. But what are *you* going to give me, Daddy?" His smile evaporated. His eyes narrowed suspiciously—you could see that he thought I was pulling some kind of stunt. But then he blushed, as though he was ashamed

35

to be thinking what he was thinking. He patted my head, and coughed and said: "Well, I thought I'd wait and let you pick out something you wanted. Is there anything particular you want?"

I reminded him of the airplane we had seen in the toy store on Canal Street. His face sagged. Oh, yes, he remembered the airplane and how expensive it was. Nevertheless, the next day I was sitting in that airplane dreaming I was zooming toward heaven while my father wrote out a check for a happy salesman. There had been some argument about shipping the plane to Alabama, but I was adamant—I insisted it should go with me on the bus that I was taking at two o'clock that afternoon. The salesman settled it by calling the bus company, who said that they could handle the matter easily.

But I wasn't free of New Orleans yet. The problem was a large silver flask of moonshine; maybe it was because of my departure, but anyway my father had been swilling it all day, and on the way to the bus station, he scared me by grabbing my wrist and harshly whispering: "I'm not going to let you go. I can't let you go back to that crazy family in that crazy old house. Just look at what they've done to you. A boy six, almost seven, talking about Santa Claus! It's all their fault, all those sour old spinsters with their Bibles and their knitting needles, those drunken uncles. *Listen* to me, Buddy. There is no God! There *is* no Santa Claus."

He was squeezing my wrist so hard that it ached. "Sometimes, oh, God, I think your mother and I, the both of us, we ought to kill ourselves to have let this happen—" (He never killed himself, but my mother did: She walked down the Seconal road thirty years ago.) "Kiss me. Please. Please. Kiss me. Tell your daddy that you love him." But I couldn't speak. I was terrified I was going to miss my bus. And I was worried about my plane, which was strapped to the top of the taxi. "Say it: 'I love you.' Say it. Please. Buddy. Say it."

It was lucky for me that our taxi-driver was a good-hearted man. Because if it hadn't been for his help, and the help of some efficient porters and a friendly policeman, I don't know what would have happened when we reached the station. My father was so wobbly he could hardly walk, but the policeman talked to him, quieted him down, helped him to stand straight, and the taxi-man promised to take him safely home. But my father would not leave until he had seen the porters put me on the bus.

Once I was on the bus, I crouched in a seat and shut my eyes. I felt the strangest pain. A crushing pain that hurt everywhere. I thought if I took off my heavy city shoes, those crucifying monsters, the agony would ease. I took them off, but the mysterious pain did not leave me. In a way it never has; never will.

Twelve hours later I was home in bed. The room

was dark. Sook was sitting beside me, rocking in a rocking chair, a sound as soothing as ocean waves. I had tried to tell her everything that had happened, and only stopped when I was hoarse as a howling dog. She stroked her fingers through my hair, and said: "Of course there is a Santa Claus. It's just that no single somebody could do all he has to do. So the Lord has spread the task among us all. That's why everybody is Santa Claus. I am. You are. Even your cousin Billy Bob. Now go to sleep. Count stars. Think of the quietest thing. Like snow. I'm sorry you didn't get to see any. But now snow is falling through the stars—" Stars sparkled, snow whirled inside my head; the last thing I remembered was the peaceful voice of the Lord telling

me something I must do. And the next day I did it. I
went with Sook to the post office and bought a penny
postcard. That same postcard exists today. It was
found in my father's safety deposit box when he died
last year. Here is what I had written him: *Hello pop
hope you are well I am and I am lurning to pedel my plain
so fast I will soon be in the sky so keep your eyes open and
yes I love you Buddy.*

Truman Capote was born in New Orleans in 1924. He spent most of his childhood in the South, but was educated at various Eastern schools. He is a member of the American Institute of Arts and Letters.